WHAT'S DIFFERENT?

Written by Melanie Zanoza

Illustrated by Art Mawhinney

Additional illustrations by the Disney Storybook Artists

Published by
Louis Weber, C.E.O., Publications International, Ltd.
7373 North Cicero Avenue, Lincolnwood, Illinois 60712

Ground Floor, 59 Gloucester Place, London W1U 8JJ

Customer Service: 1-800-595-8484 or customer_service@pilbooks.com

www.pilbooks.com

p i kids is a registered trademark of Publications International, Ltd.

Look and Find is a registered trademark of Publications International, Ltd., in the United States and in Canada.

8 7 6 5 4 3 2 1

Manufactured in China.

ISBN-13: 978-1-4127-5350-0
ISBN-10: 1-4127-5350-3

publications international, ltd.

Jasmine has sneaked out of the palace and come to the Agrabah marketplace. Here she sees all sorts of interesting things for sale. Can you find these tempting trinkets and treats? Do you see what is different?

These pistachios

This fish

 This necklace

 This copper pot

 These figs

 These dates

Snow White has met all sorts of kind animals in the forest. Can you find these caring creatures who have helped Snow White feel at home? What do you see that's different?

This turtle

This chipmunk

This squirrel
 This bird
 This rabbit
 This raccoon
 This quail

Cinderella and her prince are married and looking forward to their happily ever after. Scan the festivities for these traditional things that brought Cinderella happiness on her wedding day, then see if you can spot what is different.

Bells

Shoe

Cake Rice throw Bouquet Ring Gifts

Sebastian hopes to show Ariel just how wonderful life under the sea can be. Search the performance for the aquatic entertainers helping him make his point. What do you see that's different?

A carp playing the harp

A plaice playing the bass

 Trout rocking out

 Slugs cutting a rug

 A chub playing the tub

 A newt playing the flute

 Bass playing brass

Mulan disguised herself as a boy to take her father's place in the Chinese army. As Ping, she has met a lot of new people and creatures. Can you find these now-familiar faces in the training-camp action? Do you see what is different?

Mushu

Chi Fu

Ling

Chien-Po

Cri-Kee

Captain
Li Shang

Yao

Belle is caught up in yet another literary adventure. In fact, she's so distracted that she hasn't noticed all the wonderful things for sale in town. Can you find these merchants who are busy selling their goods? Do you see what is different?

Butcher

Baker

Bookseller Milliner Florist Farmer Barber

CHAPEAUX

Boulangerie

Café

Plantes & Fleurs

Pocahontas knows every rock and tree and creature in the forest...but do you? Look for these animals hidden along the riverbank, then see if you can spot what is different.

This bear

This turtle

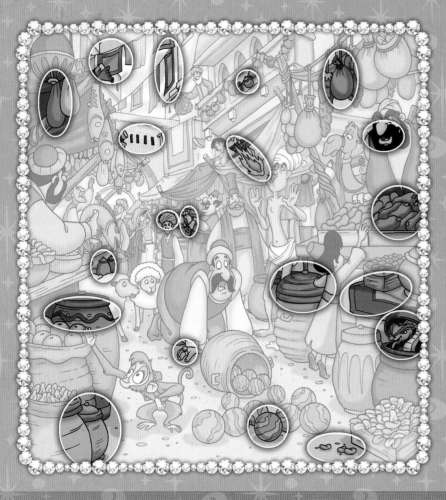

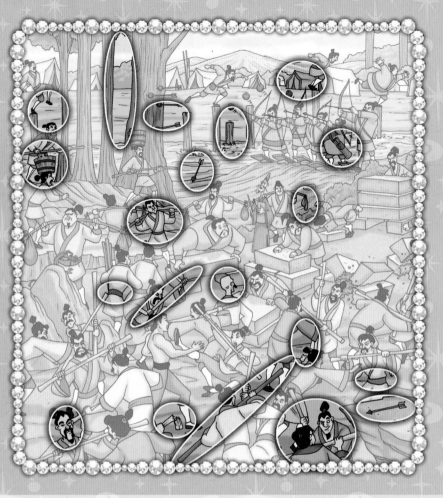